ANGRY BIRDS™

Stella

STELLA RUNS AWAY!

←STELLA is the leader of the flock. She likes things done her way, but is always on the lookout for fun!

DAHLIA is the brains of the group! Is there anything she doesn't know? The quickest way to upset her is by disturbing her experiments. →

←WILLOW loves nature and is a true artist. She dreams big but is shy, and she often keeps her ideas inside her big striped hat.

POPPY is wild, funny and she loves practical jokes! The life and soul of the gang or a total goofball, depending on your mood ...

LUCA is the baby of the bunch. He thinks he's a bigger boy than he actually is, which sometimes lands him in trouble.

GALE used to be Stella's friend, but something changed ... She started thinking she's a princess and now bosses around a gang of minion pigs.

This diary belongs to:

STELLA

....

KEEP YOUR
BEAKS OUT!

{ CONTAINS
SUPER-EXCITING AND
THRILLING STUFF! }

'Good evening, islanders! Introducing – for one night only – The Friends! Featuring Poppy on drums! Dahlia on guitar! Willow on trumpet! And the living maraca, our very own little cutie-pie, Luca! And I'm Stella, on vocals! Game onnnnn!'

CHA-CHA!

At least that's how I planned to start off our gig. OMG, I was so excited, Diary! My best friends and I – that's Willow, Dahlia, Poppy and Luca –

organised a rock concert featuring our very own band, The Friends. Our stage is kind of – how can I put this? – shaky and rickety. Dahlia built it out of random pieces of wood she found down by the stream, and it's pretty wobbly because there aren't any nails in it. While Dahlia was busy building the stage, the rest of us built audience members out of spare pieces of wood, because nobody else really lives here on the island and it would be really boring to play in front of an empty space.

Sure, Gale lives here, but she's been acting so weird lately that I wouldn't really want to invite her to anything. The pigs are a big crowd, and then there are the funny critters, but they don't know anything about music.

After we'd set everything up, it was time to go on-stage.

'This is one creaky stage,' I told Dahlia as we climbed up to play our very first gig.

'Yeah, I hope it doesn't collapse. I did my best, but I couldn't find a single nail on the whole island,' Dahlia said in a sorry voice.

'Oh well, this isn't too bad – well, it is, but it's not your fault.'

'That's right, it's not,' said Dahlia theatrically.

'It's not,' said Luca, mimicking Dahlia.

'All right, folks, it's time to turn those frowns upside down. Game on!'

At that point, I had no idea how unusual the gig would turn out to be.

'Game on!' I shouted once more. I was already on-stage when I noticed that Poppy, who was nervous about the gig, was teasing Willow. Poppy's a good friend and probably the funniest bird in the world, but she can be a pain in the tail feathers when she's feeling nervous. That's when she stops being fun – in fact, she can sometimes be a little mean. I'm sure she thinks she's still being funny. And, of course, the whole thing turned into a joke because of Poppy.

What happened was that just before we all went on-stage, Poppy whispered to Willow:

'Hey, Willow, why don't you take off that woolly hat?'

'Huh?' Willow asked in surprise from under her knitted hat.

'The audience thinks you look like a teapot with that thing on,' Poppy laughed.

'That's not funny, Poppy,' Willow snapped. Poppy was nervous, though, and this meant she didn't know when to stop.

'What? Is the kettle whistling?' Poppy giggled.

With her feelings hurt, Willow went over to mope under a tree.

'Where'd that teapot go? Is it time for tea?' Poppy continued.

'Shut your beak, Poppy!' I snapped, then went over to Willow. I'm always the one who solves other people's arguments.

'I'm not gonna play. Besides, Poppy looks like an egg,' Willow said in a miserable voice, pulling her hat down so low you couldn't see any of her.

'This is all I need,' I said angrily.

'Come on, let's go,' Dahlia shouted to us, but Willow wouldn't budge. She just kept moping under her hat.

'Apologise, Poppy, or else I'll shove you inside Willow's trumpet,' I ordered.

I glared so fiercely at Poppy, my eyes could have scorched her feathers. I roared: 'Apologise NOW, like you mean it, or I'll catapult you right into the pigs!'

Everyone stared at Poppy.

'Sorry,' she blurted out, as she saw I was about to get really mad. I get so sick of these childish arguments that I always have to solve. Sometimes Willow is too sensitive, and sometimes Poppy is too silly. Even Dahlia gets her feelings hurt because of the dumb things Poppy says. They're still my best friends, though – even if one of them's usually moping around. Mope. Mope.

The stage was swaying and creaking. It was a nice stage, but even so, I was afraid it might collapse. I was so nervous I was shaking.

'Good evening, Golden Island! Introducing – for one night only – The Friends ...' Finally I got to use my great intro.

The microphone Dahlia built kept squawking so loudly, I could see the critters who'd come to the show dropping out of the trees like overripe apples.

'One, two, three ... Game on!'

Poppy started up with some awesome drumming and, I'm telling you, Diary, it was so great! Dahlia was shredding away on her guitar, Willow blasted her trumpet and Luca was bouncing around so wildly, I had to make sure he didn't fall off the stage and into the stream flowing behind him.

The audience members bopped along with the music, and we had a fantastic time!

I felt like a star when I started to sing.

The title of the song was 'Us,' and it was about us friends: Willow, Dahlia, Luca, Poppy and, of course, me – Stella. Willow had suggested naming the song 'You' and making it about the audience so they wouldn't feel left out, but there's no way it could be called 'You' when it's about us. Sometimes Willow can be a little too nice.

What I didn't know was that during that song, we were being watched from behind a tree by my ex-best friend, Gale. I also didn't know what she was about to do.

But before I tell you that, Diary, here's our song entitled 'Us':

We're Stella, Dahlia, Poppy, Luca and Willow,
Which one's which? That's what you want to know.
Well, Willow wears a hat and loves creating art.
Dahlia can build anything – she's really
super-smart,
Poppy's always joking and likes to make some
noise!
Silly Luca mucks around, he's just a little boy.
My name's Stella, and I'm fun and happy
(drum roll) …
but I'm brave and tough when I need to be!'
(Poppy's drum solo).

Willow blasted some more notes on her trumpet, and Dahlia played so hard that the strings broke on her guitar. Luca was tuckered out after hopping around through the whole song, and my voice was almost gone.

At the end of the song, our fans just stood and stared.

'Thanks, you've been a great audience!' I shouted hoarsely into the microphone and watched as a few critters ran off into the forest.

We all felt fantastic. Then, just as we were heading off the stage, something strange happened. Something that was about to spoil the whole evening. And guess who was behind it, dear Diary?

Oh yes. Gale.

'Rubbish! Cheap, talentless rubbish! Your song was like poison to our ears!' Gale yelled and stepped out from behind her tree. As she came forwards, Gale knocked over a couple of wooden spectators, but she didn't care about them.

'Don't knock over the audience, you pig of a bird!' I shouted angrily, but Gale just barged onto the stage, followed by dozens of pigs.

Gale was wearing a shiny dress. It had a long train, which the pigs were carrying.

She wore a crown that was almost as tall as me.

'I'm blinded,' Willow said as she hid under her hat, because Gale's dress sparkled so brightly it was difficult to see anything.

Luca was teetering on the edge of the stage towards the stream, but Poppy grabbed hold of him at the last second.

'Plop,' a terrified Luca said quietly to himself.

'Gale, this is our stage. Get lost!' I ordered, but Gale wasn't listening.

'What's that little bug buzzing about?' she asked haughtily, causing the pigs to snort with laughter.

'Bring the organ!' Gale commanded, and the pigs hoisted a huge pipe organ onto the stage. The stage creaked so much, I thought it was going to come crashing down any second.

'Gale, this isn't your stage,' I repeated, but it had no effect.

Gale grabbed the microphone.

'Hey, gimme that, you pig!' I snapped, surprising one of the pigs.

'Well, we definitely are pigs. And that one's a bird, there's a tree, and there's a rock over there...' the pig pointed out sheepishly.

Gale shot the pig a look that shut him up.

'Clear those squirts out of the way,' Gale shrieked. Before I could do anything, the pigs threw us all off the stage.

Gale turned the microphone on. 'The rubbish has now been cleared away from the stage,' she sneered.

I could see Poppy getting ready to charge back up there.

'Wait – let her mess it up,' I whispered to Poppy.

'I'm a pop princess ... unbelievable ... talented ... amazing ... unbelievable ...'

'You already said unbelievable ... or are you doubly unbelievable?' Dahlia noticed, because she's very precise about these things – about everything, in fact. Gale didn't hear Dahlia's remark, though.

'... The one and only LADY GALE!' Gale shouted at the top of her lungs. The pigs nearby shielded their ears.

'I missed that. Did you say your name was Jingle Bells?' Poppy snickered. The pigs started up the organ, and it produced some very strange noises. Poppy's drumsticks rolled off the stage.

'Well?' Gale hissed to the pig next to her.

The pig leaped to attention and took the microphone.

'So then, ladies and gentlemen ...' the pig said bashfully.

'Louder – don't pussyfoot around!' Gale ordered.

The pig took a deep breath and announced: 'And now, Lady Gale will perform for you the song "Golden... uh... Treasure!"'

Some deep notes came booming out of the organ. There were at least ten different pigs playing it, with some of them bouncing around on the keyboards and others on the pedals down below. Gale moved around the stage dramatically as she warbled:

Golden treasure, I'm gonna find it
Golden treasure, where are you?
Golden treasure, nothing's gonna stop me
I'm a princess, forever and ever!
I'll soon feel the power,
Golden treasure, you're gonna be mine!

And the choreography! I could hardly watch without laughing. Gale tottered around the stage, and then suddenly a pig covered in gold sequins appeared on-stage too.

'Where do I go?' the pig whispered to Gale in the middle of the verse.

'Just stay put over there,' Gale hissed, then continued singing as she pointed to the pig:

Golden egg – I mean, treasure – there you are!

The pig almost fell over from the force of Gale's singing voice, but he played his role well.

'Hi everybody, I'm the golden egg,' the pig giggled.

'Oh, like, bravo!' Poppy yelled, as the rest of us burst out laughing.

Gale swept off the stage and disappeared along with her pig, without so much as a word to us.

'She's crazy,' Willow said once we'd recovered from Gale's unplanned performance.

'Did she say "golden egg"?' Dahlia wondered.

'Who cares about her omelette? Gale's completely cuckoo,' I said, although I was also wondering what had happened to Gale. Not too long ago, she used to be a good friend of mine, one of our gang. Then something happened to make Gale turn really weird and snotty.

And now she was bonkers too.

After the gig, we all headed over to the terrace to watch the sunset and enjoy some treats. Dahlia had set up a cheery campfire by the roots of our home tree.

'Gale spoiled the whole evening,' Willow fretted.

'It wasn't spoiled,' I said.

'Spoiled,' Luca said, gazing at the flames.

Hmph, now these guys were grumping about crazy Gale. Who cares? Let's focus on us!

'Our gig was so great, nobody's going to remember anything about Lady Gale.'

The others nodded, and then I added, 'Our performance was awesome, but this is only the beginning. Our band is gonna be famous!'

The others grinned.

'Stella, we owe it all to you. You wrote such a great song for us,' Dahlia said.

'And just think, someday we'll have dozens of songs and an awesome stage! A real stage!' I added. Their smiles were almost wide enough to cover their whole faces.

'Here's to our band,' Dahlia said, raising her glass of juice.

'To our band!' everyone chimed in, and then we partied. Danced. Laughed. Shrieked. As the evening grew darker, the campfire died down. Luca yawned and his eyelids drooped.

'Group hug!' I called out, and we all stood in a circle to hug each other.

'Willow, bring the teapot in the hat,' Poppy said. But Willow didn't mind this time.

'Quiet, mush-for-brains,' she replied, and they both laughed.

'I think we should say a friendship oath. You guys are the most precious thing in the world to me,' I said, filled with emotion.

'What's a friendship oath?' Dahlia asked.

'How about a friendship boat? A boat you go on with your friends,' Poppy joked. The thought of a friendship boat made me laugh too.

'Yes yes, very funny, Poppy. Here, take this.'

I gave each of them a glowing ember from the fire on the end of a stick.

'Hold onto these and listen closely to what I say. Then we'll tap them together,' I explained. I continued in an official tone:

'A friend is always loyal and never lies. A friend always wants to help, never to hurt. Friendship is everlasting. With these embers, we will seal our friendship forever. One, two, three!'

We tapped our embers together, and they made a nice thump in mid-air.

It was a festive atmosphere, and things felt good. That's how it is when you're good friends.

LATER

Dear Diary,

When I got home, I was planning to sleep for about a week. Or at least a couple days. Then I thought one night would be enough beauty sleep for this rock star. I got under the covers and shut my eyes.

'Snrrrrk fwww.'

I wasn't really snoring. I was just seeing what it would feel like to snore like an engine. It was hard to get to sleep when I was still so excited, and my heart was racing.

'Beep!'

What was that?

'Beep!'

There was a strange noise coming from under my bed. Eek! It was really scary. Is this what drove Gale crazy, too?

'Beep!'

Besides that weird beeping, there was a strange light shining out from under my bed. Was it a dream?

It was a machine that was making the beeps. The machine had a big green button in the middle that I pressed bravely. The machine buzzed a little, and then Dahlia's face appeared on a screen.

'Hi there,' said Dahlia.

I was totally astonished.

'Wait a sec.' Just then, the screen split into sections, and all my friends' faces appeared on the device.

'Great machine, Dahlia!' I exclaimed.

'I've been working on it for a long time,' Dahlia said proudly. 'We can use it to stay in touch with each other when we're apart.'

'Wow! You're such a great inventor, Dahlia!' I said.

'What do you call this machine?' Willow asked.

'A speaking device?' Poppy suggested.

BEEP!

'Too long,' Dahlia decided.

'A speaky?' I said.

'A speaky!' they all exclaimed.

And so the machine was called a speaky. Dahlia really is a supergenius to invent stuff like that.

We all said good night to each other. I got under the covers and shut my eyes. Then I heard Poppy's voice whispering from the speaky:

'I am the horrible Lady Gale and I'm going to perform my song, "The Bird with the Golden Egg",' Poppy giggled.

'Go to sleep, silly!' I told her and then laughed to myself as I finally fell asleep.

Band practice. Yaaaay! I thought I'd suggest we
go swimming together after practice, because
Poppy promised me she'd teach me how to dive.
I don't know how to dive, because:
1. I always open my mouth by mistake.
2. I swallow water.
3. I can't see anything.
4. I don't like diving.

I want to learn, because you can find all kinds
of stuff at the bottom of the ocean. Once Poppy
found a piece of glass that Dahlia made into a
big magnifying glass for us. The magnifying
glass concentrated the sun's rays so that when
we aimed it at the sun, we could burn designs
into the trunks of fallen trees. It was a lot of
fun. Unfortunately, Willow's hat got scorched so
badly, her whole head almost got singed, and she
was really scared. She didn't laugh at all when

Poppy joked, 'Willow's such a hothead, her hat's giving off smoke!'

The rest of us found Willow's smoking hat hilarious, but it hurt her feelings and we had to plead with her for hours to come out.

'Here I come, bubbleheads!' I called out to the girls as I approached our teetering, creaking stage.

Suddenly, Poppy leaped out in front of me from behind a tree.

'Morning, Stella, all's well that ends well, right?' Poppy asked.

'What are you talking about?' I replied as I tried to go around her, but she kept blocking my path.

'Stop right there!' Poppy ordered, spinning me around.

'What are you doing, Poppy?' I asked, as she led me firmly in the other direction.

'This way!'

'Why aren't we going on-stage? Where are you taking me?' I asked, but Poppy didn't reply.

'Say something, Poppy!'

But Poppy just chuckled strangely. I was powerless to resist.

We came to a stop by a big rock. I saw that Poppy's drum kit was already set up there.

'This is where we're rehearsing today,' Poppy announced, as she hopped up behind her drums. 'Willow and Luca are coming here too.'

'What do you think you're doing?' I asked.

'Change of scenery,' Willow replied as she and Luca appeared on cue.

'Scenery!' Luca exclaimed. I didn't feel like spoiling their fun. So we're on a big rock, I thought to myself. But where was Dahlia?

'Let's go – one, two, three!' Poppy started drumming.

'Stop, Poppy! Dahlia's not here!' I tried to say, but Poppy just kept drumming and singing over me.

'The drummer's totally the heart of the band. They're like the heart that keeps the beeeeat … No drums, no beat … everybody join in!' Poppy shrieked and drummed.

'Don't scream, Poppy! My ears hurt,' I shouted, but it was no use.

Willow and Luca started playing, too, as if it were normal that Dahlia wasn't there. Then I just lost it.

'Pipe down!' I yelled, red with rage.

Poppy's drumsticks fell off the rock.

Willow jammed her hat down to cover her head, which is her way of saying 'Do not disturb.' Luca hid behind the drums. There was complete silence.

'Ho-hum, feeling kinda tired now. I'm gonna go pick up my drumsticks and take a nap. Thanks for a good practice,' Poppy said as she got down off the rock.

'Stop, Poppy! We're gonna rehearse now,' I ordered, but Poppy didn't stop.

'I'll call you later on the speaky,' she said as she kept going.

'Poppy. Teach me to dive now. You promised,' I said. Poppy stopped.

'The thing is … um … right now, today, we can't go diving, no way,' she stammered.

'How come we can't go diving?'

Willow lifted her hat a little, and I could see her and Poppy exchange a brief glance.

'You see, we're busy and you …' Willow began, but Poppy interrupted her, poking Willow so that her hat fell down over her eyes again.

'All right, Stella. We'll teach you. What we'll do is have you count the pebbles you find around this rock,' Poppy said importantly.

'Why should I count those pebbles?' I asked.

'When you … um … dive, you should also count some pebbles, otherwise you might drown. Then you go in after them. I'll go get the diving area ready,' Poppy said, then hurried off down the path and out of sight. Willow also hopped off, taking Luca with her.

'See ya, Stella,' Willow said quietly as she left.

What a strange explanation. I was kind of surprised, but then again, I don't really know much about diving. I looked at the pebbles.

One, two, three, thirty. Bah, I'm Stella, not some dumb pebble counter! I had been counting pebbles for maybe five seconds when I decided I'd had enough.

'Poppy's a mean liar,' I grumbled, swiping the pebbles off the rock in rage.

I was really fuming when I went up and knocked on Poppy's door.

I could hear strange buzzing noises. There was whispering and the sound of papers rustling inside. I knocked again.

Knock knock knock!

Poppy came to the door, looking very sleepy.

'Oh, Stella, is it morning already?' she asked, yawning.

'It's evening now. Explain to me how counting pebbles is related to diving!' I snapped.

Poppy laughed.

'It's not, I remembered wrong. Sorry, I'm going to bed now,' she said and started to shut the door. Then I spotted Luca peeking out from behind the door.

'Luca!' I said in surprise.

'Luca!' he said, before someone grabbed him and pulled him back inside.

'Why is Luca in there?' Just then I saw Dahlia and Willow reflected in a drinking glass. 'What are you guys doing in there?' I asked.

'I'm going to bed, Stella,' Poppy said and shut the door.

'You meanies! How come I wasn't invited?' I asked angrily, but Poppy managed to shut the door.

'There's nobody here, Stella. You're imagining things. Bye-bye – now I'm gonna get my beauty sleep,' Poppy shouted through the door.

'Liar!' I screamed at the top of my lungs.

Once I got home, I simmered down, because:
1. Maybe Poppy really was going to bed.

2. Maybe I just thought I saw the other girls.
3. Poppy is my friend and wouldn't lie to me.

I washed up and took out my speaky. I pressed the red button and yelled into it, 'Hey friends, are you there?'

Nobody answered. They must have already fallen asleep.

So I went to sleep too and dreamed about millions of pebbles teasing me: 'Stella doesn't have any friends, Stella doesn't have any friends!' Luckily, it was only a dream. I have awesome friends – you can tell that by the friendship oath we made.

Unbelievable! This is completely ridiculous!

I found a note outside my door that said, 'Good morning, Stella. Today we're going to rehearse at the top of the biggest tree on the island.'

You can't rehearse in a tree.

Like *duhhh*.

No. I'll try to keep a positive attitude here. Maybe Willow, with her artistic mindset, wants to try out some different places. And you do get nice views from a tree.

LATER

Well. I have no words to describe what happened. Still, I'll try to get the whole weird episode down in writing.

When I arrived at the base of the biggest tree on the island, I saw Poppy, Dahlia and Luca already on a big branch near the top.

'Hey, friends, I'm on my way up!' I called out, and then they all started acting really weird. They didn't look excited the way they normally do when they see a friend. They looked like they were hiding something.

'Oh, hi,' Dahlia said in a flat voice.

'Where's Willow?' I asked, once I had reached the top.

'Over there, asleep,' Poppy pointed down and gave an odd fake smile.

Willow's hat was way off at the edge of the forest.

'Let's wake her up. We've got band practice now,' I said.

But Dahlia had other ideas. 'Let Willow sleep if she's tired,' she said. 'We'll practise the parts where she's not needed.'

How lazy, I thought. 'OK, she can sleep. But only for a little while. Where are the

instruments?' I asked, but Poppy was looking at the others and Dahlia was fidgeting with some leaves. Luca was pretending to be a leaf, hanging and swinging from a branch.

'The what?' Dahlia asked, as if she hadn't heard my question.

'The instruments!' I was starting to get irritated.

'Oh … yeah,' Dahlia said.

I saw Poppy nudge Dahlia. 'Tell her,' she whispered.

'Tell me what?' I asked.

Dahlia blushed. Finally, she said, 'The thing is, if you think about all the strains on a bird's health, like, if we practise every day, your feathers might fall out, and …' Dahlia explained with a strange expression on her face.

'Yeah, what Dahlia's trying to say is, shouldn't we take a day off?' Poppy asked, still smiling that weird smile, with her mouth open so wide that a fly actually flew in there and then flew back out, shaking its head.

'Willow, wake up! These guys up here are going on about taking a day off,' I shouted as I got down from the tree.

'Don't wake her up!' Poppy shrieked after me, but I didn't pay any attention, because night-time is for sleeping.

'Wake up!' I nudged the sleeping Willow ... but it wasn't Willow! It was just a heap of moss with a hat on top!

And it wasn't even Willow's hat – it was somebody else's.

'Where's Willow, and what's going on here?' I demanded.

Poppy cautiously came over to where I was standing.

'Oh, if only we knew. And if only we knew where the sun came from or why water is wet or why trees have leaves, and not birds that look like Luca,' she babbled.

'Let's call Willow on the speaky,' I said, but Dahlia, who had just come down out of the tree, butted in.

'The line's not working today. It's too cloudy,' she said.

'But there aren't any clouds,' I said.

'You see, there are extremely rare invisible clouds in the sky today,' Dahlia began.

'Yeah, that's it. Everybody knows that,' Poppy added.

'What are you talking about?' I shouted angrily.

'Ahem … ahem … cough, cough,' Dahlia coughed and went to lie down on the ground with her eyes closed.

'What's wrong with you?' I asked in alarm.

'I think I'm coming down with something,' Dahlia said weakly.

'I'll take Dahlia home to rest,' Poppy said brightly, and I thought I saw Dahlia wink at Poppy, but maybe it was just a symptom of her illness.

'I'll come too,' I said, but Poppy resisted.

'No, don't,' she said. 'It's better if the infection doesn't spread to everybody. You stay here with Luca.'

And then they were gone. I just stood there with Luca, feeling like a prat. I've never felt so dumb before. It's not often I am lost for words, but my friends' behaviour had been so weird that I somehow just froze.

Back home, I sat and thought about our band rehearsals over the past few days. There have been some strange things going on:
1. Our rehearsal times have been really weird.
2. Our rehearsal spaces have been really weird.
3. My friends have been acting really weird.

What's going on here? It might be because:
1. They don't like me anymore.
2. They want to be friends with each other, but not with me.

We just said that friendship oath recently. How can my best friends seem as weird as Gale all of a sudden? I shouldn't think about terrible things like that. Of course they're my friends.

I drank my evening cup of tea and took my speaky out from under the bed. I pressed the button and chirped into it.

'Yoo-hoo, any friends out there? It's me, Stella.'

Nobody seemed to be on the line.

'Hey, friends! It's Stella calling,' I added, and then the device crackled. I could hear some unclear voices coming through.

'Don't answer!'

'I pressed it by accident ... Shhh ...'

I could hear some odd noises and tapping.

'Luca, Poppy, Willow, Dahlia?' I called out, because along with the tapping I thought I could hear all their voices.

'Stella, it's Dahlia here. How's it going? I hope we won't get cut –'

The line was cut off.

Silence.

HELLO?

'Hello? Dahlia?' But there was no sound from the speaky. How weird. Was it broken? Maybe there was a problem on the line, causing the random sounds …

A LITTLE LATER

I woke up from a deep sleep to hear my name being called through the speaky.

'Stella! Stellaaaa!' Poppy called.

'Are you there, Stella?' Dahlia's voice asked.

I didn't feel like getting out of bed, because I'd been asleep and was feeling miserable.

'Is that S, is that T, is that E, is that L, is that L …' I heard Poppy joking into the speaky, but I switched it off and pulled the covers over my ears. I didn't feel like talking to them.

I went to sleep and had a nightmare about Gale. I had transformed into Gale's talking crown and could only say, 'Is that S, T, E, L, L, A, I, S, D, U, M, B?'

And then I woke up in a cold sweat.

OK, today really was the final straw.

I mean it.

I was just getting up and ready when there was a knock at my door. It had to be Poppy, because her knock sounds so silly. Not a regular knock-knock-knock, more like knockityknockityknockity. Sort of like a little creature scampering up and down the door – it's pretty weird.

Knockityknockityknockity, the insistent knocks continued.

I opened the door.

'Good morning, Stella. You still have your nightie on,' Poppy exclaimed in the doorway.

'Morning. You noticed. What is it?'

'It it it. That's just it. What if, if it's about "it," we could just say "it," when somebody asks what it is?' Poppy giggled.

'Bye,' I said, about to close the door, but Poppy barged in.

'Wait, I do have something to talk about,' she said.

I went over to take off my nightie, and Poppy followed me.

'What are you planning to do today, Stella?' Poppy enquired.

'Go watch the butterflies, and then go swimming. Wanna come along? You could teach me how to dive today,' I suggested.

'No, don't go. And I'm not going to teach you,' Poppy replied and plunked herself down on the sofa.

'Why shouldn't I go, and why won't you teach me?' I wondered out loud.

'The thing is, I just bumped into the others and we decided to play a game today, like, "Who can stay in their own home the longest?"' she said.

'I've never heard of a game like that,' I replied.

'It's super-popular,' Poppy claimed, her eyes bright as she grabbed the slice of buttered bread I had made for myself off the table.

'You greedy gobbler. Where is it played?' I asked.

'Here, on the island,' Poppy replied.

'Who else plays it?' I asked.

'Lots of animals. The critters, for example. They play it every day,' Poppy said.

'That may well be, but it sounds like a really boring game,' I said as I packed my butterfly net into my bag.

'Dahlia was right,' Poppy sighed.

'About what?' I asked.

Poppy stared off into the distance.

'Even though you're braver than all of us, you don't like challenging games that require strength of character,' she explained.

That made me mad. What was she talking about? I can do anything. After all, I'm Stella!

'Of course I can do it!' I snapped at Poppy.

'Awesome!' Poppy exclaimed. 'Let's see how it goes. The first one who leaves their home today is the loser. Time starts now,' Poppy shouted and ran towards her own home.

I sat nervously on the sofa. This might be a really dumb game, but the good thing was that we were finally doing something together. Sort of. I tried to come up with something to do. First I counted the pictures on my curtains. There were one hundred and twenty in all. Then I got down on the floor and pretended to be a rug, but it's pretty boring being a rug.

'Bleahh,' I said, and got up.

Then I pretended to be a curtain, opening and closing, opening and closing in front of the window.

'Double-bleahh.' That was even more boring. And it was still only morning. This was going to be a really long, boring day, but I wasn't going to be the one to lose at this game.

In the end, I decided to pass the time by writing a poem. Here's what I came up with:

Stella's my name; I'm playing a game.
There's no chance you'll beat me, 'cos I rule
*   completely.*
The best bird's no fella; she's a brave girl named
*   Stella.*
My gameplay's not sloppy – I won't lose to Poppy.

Isn't it awesome? I might suggest it as our next song. Willow's such an artistic bird, she'd be able to appreciate my poem, but I can't take it and show it to her yet because of this game. I'll show her later.

Then I drew a picture of Poppy. Here's how it turned out:

'Triple-bleahh – there's nothing to do!' I sighed. Then I remembered I have a telescope. Dahlia gave it to me for my birthday. I could use it to look outside! Yesss! I aimed the telescope at the window. According to the rules of the game, this was totally allowed, because I wasn't leaving my home, just looking out.

Looking at stuff with the telescope was really fun. I focused it on the ocean and watched as the waves hit the shore. I focused it in the direction of Gale's fortress and saw her bossing the poor pigs around. Of course, I couldn't hear what Gale was saying, but the pigs were just looking down meekly at the ground, while Gale was really acting like their ruler.

Then I pointed the telescope at the edge of the forest, where I saw Poppy. She was smiling and looked really happy. But she was outside! What's more, when I moved the telescope, I also saw Willow and Dahlia. And sure enough, Luca was there, too! I watched through the telescope as all my friends stood in a semicircle around a big tree, laughing. That made me furious!

Had they lied to me about this dumb game so I wouldn't interrupt them playing? I was outraged. I looked again. Now there was a picture hanging in the tree. It was a picture of ME – and what's more, it was a cartoon! There was some kind of rag drawn over my eyes! My so-called friends had tricked me into staying home today so they could be together. On top of that, they drew a cartoon of me, and now they were laughing at it.

'WHAT ARE YOU DOING, YOU TRAITORS?!' I screamed at the top of my lungs from my window, but of course they couldn't hear me.

I got down out of our home tree onto the ground and dashed over to the edge of the forest – where I'd seen them poking fun at me. But when I got there, everybody was gone. Even the picture was no longer in the tree.

I raced over to Willow's place and banged on the door.

'Stella? You lost the game,' she said.

'You dirty rotten liars! I saw you guys outside!' I was so mad, I was ready to explode.

Willow looked really uneasy.

'I'm painting a picture right now. I don't have time to talk,' she said, then closed the door and locked it.

'Coward!' I yelled.

Then I ran over to Dahlia's door and barged inside.

'Stella! Did you give up?' Dahlia said, looking up from her book.

'I saw you all around the tree, laughing at me!' I fumed.

I was so furious, I grabbed Dahlia's pillow and ripped it to shreds. The stuffing floated in the air, making it look like there was a snowstorm in Dahlia's home.

'How come you ripped up my pillow?' Dahlia asked, covered in white fluff.

'Why did you lie to me?' I yelled, my eyes flashing with rage.

AARGH!

Dahlia filled her kettle and put it on the hob. 'Calm down, Stella. I know what this is about,' she said.

'Start explaining, or I'll tear your whole place to shreds,' I threatened, still furious.

Dahlia calmly took the kettle off the stove and poured two cups of tea for us.

'Did you know that we birds have brains that can start to see supernatural visions if we spend all day at home?' Dahlia said. She slurped her tea.

'Is that true?' I asked.

'Of course,' Dahlia said in a convincing tone.

Hmm ... Maybe Dahlia was telling the truth. She is a very wise bird. Besides, friends aren't that nasty to each other. I started to calm down.

'That's how our brains are constructed. Would you like another cup of tea?' she asked.

'Yes, thanks. Sorry about wrecking your pillow,' I replied.

'That's all right. It was almost like it was snowing,' Dahlia laughed. I felt so much better after talking to Dahlia.

A LITTLE LATER

That evening, I called the others on the speaky.

'It's Stella here. Are you guys there?' I asked.

The device crackled a lot, but eventually I heard the others' voices.

'Hi Stella,' said Willow.

'I'm here,' Dahlia chimed in.

'Are we having band practice tomorrow?' I asked.

There was a long silence.

'Uh … sure,' Dahlia said.

'Yeah, but on the beach, OK?' Poppy asked.

'Why there?' I wondered.

'Because I want to see if I can drum the water. And then we can go diving later on,' Poppy said.

'Sure, great,' I said. At last, I'd get to learn how to dive.

'Great,' Luca chirped.

'Bye,' Dahlia said, but there was so much crackling on the line I could barely hear her.

'See you tomorrow,' I could just make out Willow's words.

I turned off my speaky and went to bed. Tomorrow is going to be an awesome day. Right?

Wrong. Today hasn't been an awesome day at all.

This morning, as I made my way to the beach for band practice, I thought how nice it was that I visited Dahlia at her place for tea last night. I was in a better mood, and I had convinced myself that all that other horrible stuff was definitely just my imagination. I whistled a happy tune as I went down the path towards the beach.

When I got to the beach, there was nobody there.

'Girls?!' I shouted, but I couldn't see a soul.

Furious, I went back home. My friends were up to something behind my back, and they kept lying to me. I felt like such a fool.

I gave myself four choices:

1. Give in. I could give in to the situation and let them scheme among themselves.

2. Become a hermit. That is, stay home alone all the time and quit the band. I'd stay here until I got old, coming to terms with what good friends the others are to each other, and how much fun they have without me. That would be a little awkward, because we all live in the same tree, but they'd soon get used to the fact I never left my own treehouse.

3. Blow a fuse. I could go ballistic at the others. This one felt like a very appealing option. But: blowing a fuse might feel good, but then what? They'd keep doing the same thing, and I'd just be more unhappy than before.

4. Leave. I could leave and find some better company.

I thought about it for a little while – at *least* four seconds. I decided I would leave.

I packed my most valued possessions in my backpack and looked around my house one last time. I was going to miss it and our tree, but Stella's gotta do what Stella's gotta do.

'Thanks for everything, Home. This girl's off to start a new life. Game on!' I said.

I opened the door. To my surprise, Dahlia, Willow, Luca and Poppy were all standing right there.

'What are you doing here, traitors?' I growled.

'Traitors? What do you mean?' Willow wondered.

'You know very well,' I said, going out the door.

'We came to get you for practice. Let's go to our stage,' Dahlia said.

'Have a nice time,' I sneered and continued on my way.

'Why is all your furniture covered with sheets?' Willow asked, peeking inside.

'And why do you have a big backpack?' Poppy asked.

Were they stupid as well as mean?

'I'm leaving now, and I'm not coming back,' I said decisively and then got down out of the tree.

'Where are you actually going?' Willow asked in surprise.

'Oh, she'll be back by dinnertime,' Poppy laughed, but Dahlia shushed her.

'I think Stella's actually serious,' Dahlia said and came running after me. 'Where are you going?' she asked.

'To find a new life,' I said dramatically, giving them all a quick wave before I headed towards the gloomy forest.

'Don't go, Stella,' Dahlia said. There were tears in her eyes, but I didn't care.

'Bye-bye, see ya around, or maybe not. Game on!' I yelled and ventured into the forest.

At the start of my journey, I hid and looked back, where I saw the girls watching me, their eyes wide. Willow was crying. Luca was crying because Willow was crying. Poppy was clearly cracking a joke, but Dahlia gave her a stern look. There might even have been a tear in the corner of Poppy's eye, too.

Well, that was that. Let them have all the fun they wanted together. Oh, they'll come to regret lying, I thought to myself. Only after I'd set out did I realise just how gloomy the forest was. The tree branches swayed and looked like huge arms trying to grab hold of me. I don't get scared very often, but I was a little scared now. There were strange rustling sounds coming from the forest too, but I tried not to let them get to me. I reminded myself that I'm Stella the brave! Some forest can't scare me. And what choice did I have? I couldn't go back, because then the girls would have just made fun of me.

Then I heard a loud *creeeak!* I jumped behind a big shrub to hide. Now I was pretty scared. There was nothing to do but to run really fast towards the beach, where I'd be able to see the ocean and get away from the dense, gloomy forest.

I tried to remember which way the beach was and ran pell-mell with my eyes shut. I ran and ran, but never reached the beach. When I opened my eyes, I saw to my horror that I'd gotten lost even deeper in the forest. I tried my very best to stay strong. No, Stella, don't be afraid, I thought, you can handle anything!

I had packed my speaky in my backpack, too. I took it out, and for a second, I thought about calling the others for help, but just as I was about to press the green button, I had second thoughts. I remembered how the others had acted. I put the speaky back in my backpack.

I'm Stella the brave! I thought, and continued on my way. Fear would be my companion. At least it didn't run off or tell lies.

'So, Fear, which way to the beach?'

It seemed like one of the branches in the gloomy forest was pointing the way. I decided to trust it – I didn't have any other choice.

'Thanks, Fear, I'll go that way,' I said in a calm voice, although I didn't feel calm at all.

LATER

I'd been on the go for a really long time, and it was getting darker and darker. Suddenly, I saw some little specks of light ahead. Were they fireflies? Maybe they could become my new gang of friends. Then I realised they weren't fireflies but lights. What was going on here so late at night? I hid behind a rock.

I heard a voice giving orders.

'One, two, three, four. That's the pace! One, two, three, four! Move it, you lazy good-for-nothings!'

The voice was familiar, and it was coming from where the lights were. Just then, one of the lights illuminated who was doing the shouting.

'Gale?' I blurted out accidentally.

Everyone froze.

'Stop digging!' Gale ordered. Then I saw a bunch of sweaty pigs wearing headlamps and holding shovels. Gale was standing in front of them, wearing a crown and a long gown.

'Who's there?' Gale demanded, gesturing to one of the guard pigs to inspect my hiding place.

I knew then that I'd be discovered, so I emerged from behind the rock. 'Hi Gale,' I said.

'Stella? What are you doing here in the middle of the night?' Gale asked.

The guard pig approached me with a big, huge net, but Gale halted him with a small gesture.

'Oh, what's a bird doing in the forest in the middle of the night,' I tried to laugh casually, because I didn't want Gale to know why I'd left the others. I don't trust her one inch.

'Well, tell me,' Gale continued.

I made up a fib on the spot: 'I'm trying to look for my backpack in the dark.'

'Huh?' Gale snapped in disbelief.

'Huh?' echoed the crowd of pigs.

'Yep. It's handy, because sometimes when it's too bright in the daytime, I can go out in the

dark,' I explained, and then quickly changed the subject. 'So, how come you're all digging out here in the middle of the night?'

The pigs looked at each other, and then at Gale. Gale thought for a moment, and then said, 'We're not digging,' she laughed cheerlessly.

'You *were* digging! I saw you,' I insisted.

Gale thought some more and then said, 'I lost my house keys. We're searching for them here.'

I saw that some of the holes the pigs had dug were filling with water. And there were tons of holes everywhere. 'You can't dig this much,' I told them. 'You'll make the island sink,' I told Gale in horror.

Gale laughed arrogantly.

'Hah! Nonsense. Oh, look! Here are my keys,' she said, pointing at the ground. She bent to pick something up.

Somehow, seeing Gale felt nice and safe. Even though she'd got really strange, I was no longer alone in the horrible forest. I'm sure Gale had missed me too, because she asked me to spend the night at her place.

I thought it over for a moment. My options were:

1. Spend the night in the forest.
2. Spend the night in one of the holes dug by the pigs.
3. Go back home.
4. Go to Gale's place for the night.

Yep. The last one was the best option.

'Yeah, I can come,' I said, relieved at being able to go to a safe place for the night. In the morning, I'd be able to continue on my way and find myself some new friends. In daylight I'd be able to see things, but now I couldn't even see my own eyelashes.

'Yay! Let's have a sleep-over!' Gale squealed.

'Yay, sleep-over!' the pigs shouted and put down their shovels, but clammed up when Gale glared at them.

'You're not coming, you green idiots. You're staying here to pick...' Gale glanced at me for a

second. '... your noses,' she continued. Just then,
some of the pigs started shoving things up their
noses. Out of the corner of my eye, I could see
the pig in charge of the digging wink at Gale, but
I didn't care. I was finally going to get out of the
forest.

AT NIGHT

As Gale and I went to her place, we chatted about
all kinds of nice things. A little different from
my situation a few minutes earlier, when I was

wandering alone in the forest, dodging tree branches.

Gale's new home is a castle located right next to a volcano. It's a big difference from her old home in the tree. Every wall has mirrors and huge crowns on it. An enormous chandelier in the shape of a crown hangs from the ceiling. The lights seem to follow Gale wherever she went inside the castle.

'Lots of crowns,' I remarked to Gale.

'I think they're marvellous,' Gale replied as she found some pyjamas for us.

'With those points on them, you could use them to roast sausages around a campfire,' I suggested, and we giggled as we sat on the floor. It was really nice to be with Gale after so long. Now she was just normal, not a liar like Poppy and those guys.

We tried on different fancy outfits and pretended to be queens. I was Queen Stella the First, and Gale was Queen Gale the First.

Not very imaginative, I know, but neither of us wanted to be the Second.

Then we covered Gale's mirrors in toothpaste, which distorted our reflections in really weird ways. In one mirror, I looked just like a white pig, and Gale looked just like Poppy. I haven't laughed so much in a really long time. This was exactly the kind of friendship I'd been missing.

Then we sprawled out on Gale's huge bed and talked about everything.

'What's Willow up to these days?' Gale asked.

'She draws and writes a lot,' I replied.

Even though I was on good terms with Gale now, I didn't want to tell her anything about our argument.

'I think Willow's kind of artsy-fartsy,' Gale said. Then she continued in a nasty tone, 'And that Poppy is really irritating. She thinks she's so funny, but she's really not.'

I stuck up for Poppy. 'She does have some pretty good jokes,' I told Gale.

Gale just carried on, not listening to me. 'And what about that Test Tube Dahlia? She's such a know-it-all. Who can stand that?' Gale yapped.

I started to feel furious. Even though the girls had let me down, I didn't want to be mean to them.

Gale kept up her hateful spiel: 'And then there's that blue baby. He's such a dum-dum, it's a miracle he hasn't already gotten lost in the forest.'

'Luca's just little ...' I tried to explain, but Gale was in full flow.

'And what about your band? Stella, even you know it's rubbish. You should join Lady Gale's backing group – then you'll get to play real music,' Gale raved, but I'd had enough.

How did our sleep-over suddenly turn into this? Nobody insults our band!

I got off the bed.

'Shut your beak, Gale!'

'Now, don't get mad, Stella,' Gale said, but I didn't want to stay any longer.

'I ought to head back to the others now. It'll be morning soon,' I said.

'Don't go – let's talk some more,' Gale begged, but I didn't want to look at her silly face anymore.

'And you should stop that digging,' I said, remembering that.

'Oh, don't nag, Stella,' Gale said.

Then something happened. The rays of the morning sun flooded in and reflected off the smeared mirrors and onto me. I was bathed in the yellow morning sunlight. Gale suddenly looked odd. She glanced at the mirror and started talking gibberish.

'Mmmm ... the Golden ... Egg ...'

'What are you saying?' I wondered. I saw myself in one of the messy mirrors. I looked just like a golden ball.

I tried to escape through the door, but Gale roared, 'Pigs! Lock the door!'

I heard the door being bolted.

'Gale! Let me out!' I yelled.

'Quiet!' Gale ordered, her eyes flashing with anger.

'Let me out this instant!' I ordered Gale, but she looked like she'd gone completely crazy.

'You cannot prevent me from getting my golden treasure. I'm going to be a princess! A real, live princess! And then I'm going to banish all of you from this island,' Gale continued her strange monologue. I was terrified. This wasn't the Gale that used to be my best friend.

I looked around for an escape route. The window! It was open. I raced towards the window, but Gale shoved me into an old cage by the wall. Gale pushed the door of the cage closed and turned the key.

'Let me out of here!' I yelled, but Gale didn't seem to be listening.

'Never! You'd spoil everything,' Gale shrieked.

'I won't tell anybody you're digging up the island,' I fibbed, because of course I would tell.

But Gale just ordered the pigs to open the door and hurried out of the room.

'Time to dig, my piggies!' I heard Gale say.

'Yes, princess!' the pigs replied. Then I could hear their oinks and squeals getting farther away.

I started to wonder how I could get out of there. The speaky was in my backpack, but there was no way I could get hold of it, because Gale had hung it up on the coat rack. Was this how I was going to live for the rest of my days? I had no way of getting the door unlocked. How was I ever going to get out? Stupid, stupid Stella, I told myself.

When morning came, I was completely exhausted from bashing myself against the door of the cage. It hadn't budged.

What did Gale have up her sleeve?

The door opened.

'Good morning, dear Stella. How are things?' Gale asked as she glanced at my cage.

'Let me out of here, you pigbrain,' I snarled.

Gale took a step back.

'Never! I'm going to be a princess, and you're going to be a prisoner until the end of your miserable life. Nobody will prevent us from digging. Not even you,' she declared.

'Let me out!' I was so mad, I felt as if I was about to explode.

'I don't want to have some pipsqueak here, stopping me from digging,' Gale said. Then I saw something out of the window. It looked like it could have been Poppy, but I didn't get a good look, because they disappeared when Gale turned towards the window. Had the girls come to save me? Luckily, Gale didn't see anything. She put on an eye mask and got into bed.

'Now it's time for the princess's beauty sleep,' she said.

'You sleep during the day?' I asked.

Then there was a knock on the door.

Knock-knock-knock.

'Pigs, I told you I'm not to be disturbed during my beauty sleep!' Gale said in annoyance, turning over onto her side.

Knock-knock-knock.

'You should answer the door. Maybe it's your golden treasure,' I said, hoping it might be my rescuer.

Knock-knock-knock.

Gale was clearly obsessed by the possibility of it being her golden treasure, so she got out of bed and answered the door. There was nobody there.

'Who's bothering me?' Gale demanded. Then something rolled through the doorway. I saw Luca, wrapped in a white sheet with his face covered in mud. There was a note attached: 'I am an orphan. Please take me in.'

'Goo goo,' Luca babbled.

Gale stared at Luca, but she didn't seem to recognise him. I saw Willow from the window and tried to suppress a tweet of relief. They had come to save me! Genius. With Luca's help, I'd be able to get the key off the hook where it was hanging. Gale looked at Luca and thought for a moment.

'Maybe you could train this kid to be your servant in the palace, your highness,' I fawned. Gale's face brightened.

'Goo goo ga ga,' Luca babbled. I was proud of him. Luca was good at playing a baby.

Gale looked at Luca as if she were sizing him up.

'Good idea. I'm gonna do that,' Gale declared.

'Ga ga,' Luca gurgled and smiled at me.

'Now I'm going to sleep, so be quiet, baby,' Gale ordered and got under the covers. Luca rolled over to me.

'Luca, take the key off the hook,' I whispered to him. In his swaddling clothes, Luca rolled over underneath the row of hooks and turned his head.

'Come over here,' I whispered. Luca bounced over to me.

Gale turned onto her other side. Now we had to be careful so she wouldn't wake up.

'I guess you can't reach,' I told Luca.

'Goo goo,' Luca accidentally said out loud. Gale almost woke up.

'A golden servant ... ooh,' she mumbled in her sleep.

The girls hadn't thought things through. No way could Luca reach the hook. Impossible. I saw the girls discussing things animatedly through the window.

'Luca, you'd better get out of here before Gale figures out who you really are,' I whispered. Luca nodded. Then he picked up speed and bounced around like a rubber ball, bashing the door open in the process. I saw Poppy was already about to rush in, but Luca's noise woke Gale up.

'Ho-hum. Now, where's that baby? Oh, never mind,' Gale yawned. Poppy hid, because the pigs were hurrying in now that Gale was awake.

'Check it out, the nutcase is up,' I said under my breath.

'What?' she asked.

'I said, good morning! Or should I say afternoon,' I said sweetly.

'Ah, I had some sweet dreams,' a sleepy Gale said as she rubbed her eyes and the pigs bustled in with her breakfast.

'Plus, afternoon is the best time to let your former best friend out of jail,' I said in an attempt to take advantage of Gale's drowsiness.

'You're here to keep me company, hahahahaaa,' Gale laughed. While she ate, she tried on several different crowns.

'Dummy,' I grumbled to myself.

'Which crown should I wear today?' Gale wondered aloud, though she might have secretly wished I would help her choose. That's how Gale has always been.

I glanced at the window, but couldn't glimpse any of the girls. I thought, somebody, come up with a plan, quick! It was unbearable sitting there in that cage. I also wondered how the girls had managed to find me. Had they followed me into the forest?

'And now get to work digging, piggies,' Gale said, once she found a crown she liked.

Just then, someone knocked on the door again.

Knockityknockityknockity. It sounded a lot like Poppy.

'Line up, pigs!' Gale barked as she opened the door. But there was a strange figure standing at the door. The figure was wearing dirty ragged clothes, with some kind of cloth tied around its face.

The stranger coughed and said in a gruff voice, 'I am a beggar. May I please have a glass of water? I haven't had anything to drink in a week.' Then I saw a drumstick underneath the tattered clothes. It was Poppy! So this was their new plan. Poppy would be able to reach the hook with her drumstick and get this stupid lock open.

'I don't have time. You can drink from the ocean if you're thirsty,' Gale said as she tried to close the door, but Poppy didn't give up.

'It's so salty, that sea-water, it just makes me thirsty again,' she said.

'Oh dear. I guess you're out of luck,' Gale said and closed the door.

But Poppy still didn't give up.

'How about if I sing for you, and you pay me with a glass of water?' she suggested to Gale.

'Don't you know who I am?' Gale asked, surprising Poppy.

'Gale?' she asked quietly.

'Shhhh,' I gestured to Poppy so she wouldn't reveal her identity.

'How'd you know my name? I don't know any beggars,' Gale said.

'You're either Rita, Helen, Gale, Kevin or Olivia, but those are just guesses,' Poppy spluttered to cover herself.

Gale did a grand pirouette in satisfaction.

'When I perform, I am Lady Gale, and if anyone's going to sing here, it's me,' Gale said. Then she launched into a song at the top of her voice.

The cloth in front of Poppy's face fluttered from the force of Gale's singing, and one of her drumsticks fell to the floor. I gestured to Poppy that she should straighten out the cloth over her face so Gale wouldn't recognise her.

'Can I tell you a joke? If I make you laugh, then can I have a glass of water?' Poppy tried again after Gale was done singing.

Gale thought for a moment.

'Well, I guess I don't have anything to lose, but I bet I won't laugh,' she said.

Poppy took a deep breath and began.

'What does a pig put on its bruises?' she asked.

'Well?' Gale asked.

Poppy thought for a few seconds and then said, 'Oinkment,' Poppy laughed at her own joke. Gale was completely silent.

Oh no, what a terrible joke. Gale looked at Poppy.

'I don't get it,' Gale said.

'Oinkment ... as in ointment ... only pigs go oink ...' Poppy explained, but Gale interrupted her.

'All right, you'll get your water ...' she said.

What in the world? That was a terrible joke, and Gale didn't even laugh.

Then Gale pushed Poppy, who was revelling in her victory, away from the door and shouted after her.

'... From the ocean, you awful beggar comedian!'

Then I saw Willow through the window. We exchanged unhopeful glances. How were they going to get me out of there, when all their plans seemed to be going wrong?

'When I move into my new palace, there'll be no more banging on the door. Only the servants will open it,' Gale declared.

'What do you mean, new palace?' I asked.

'When I find my treasure, I'll be unbeatable,' she explained.

I heard her order a guard pig to stand outside the door. Before that, Gale had checked that the window was firmly shut, too.

'If anybody opens that window, a hundred pigs will turn up,' Gale threatened.

It was impossible to escape. I needed to come up with another plan, and fast.

I stayed up all night, but Gale didn't return
overnight or even the next morning. My
thoughts turned gloomy. Why weren't the other
girls even trying to help? I was going to go crazy
in my tiny cell. Maybe the girls had decided they
couldn't do anything and left to do their own
thing.

I was feeling sleepy, so I decided to take a
little snooze. After all, I wasn't going to come up
with a master plan when I was tired.

RRRRR!!!! I heard a loud scraping noise. I
snapped to attention and looked at the window.
Something made of metal was coming through
the windowpane. At the end of it, I saw Dahlia,
who was wearing protective goggles. She was
drilling a small hole through the window. But
what on earth was Dahlia planning to do with
that hole?

RRRRR!!!! the drill popped through, and I was worried Gale would come back or the guard pig would hear the sound of the drill.

'Stella,' Dahlia whispered through the hole.

'What are you doing, Dahlia?' I asked.

Dahlia peered through the hole.

'Is it really bad in there?' she asked.

'Shhh, don't let the guard pig hear,' I told her.

'Oh yeah,' she said.

'Get me out of here. I'm going crazy, and Gale is digging dangerous holes everywhere,' I said, fearing I could hear footsteps. Fortunately, the guard pig didn't come in.

'I've done some calculations on how I can get a long stick through this hole and over to that hook and then pass the keys to you,' Dahlia whispered.

Dahlia is so careful with her maths. This sounded like a good option.

'Do it!' I said.

Dahlia pushed a stick through the hole. It fit just fine. Then she carefully pointed the stick towards the row of hooks on the wall. My heart stopped as it hit a flowerpot along the way, which Dahlia hadn't included in her calculations. The pot wobbled and made a noise. The guard pig heard it too and came rushing back towards us.

'What's the prisoner up to?' the pig asked when he came in.

Don't look up and see the stick, I thought, but then I remembered pigs are simpletons.

'Nothing to worry about here. I'm suffering in prison and wobbling like a flowerpot,' I said, showing him how I wobbled, and making a noise like the flowerpot had just made.

'Huh. Well, keep it down,' the guard pig grunted. I hoped he wouldn't notice the stick.

Dahlia was watching from outside the window. She was so terrified, her goggles were all steamed up.

'You're a great guard, by the way,' I said.

The pig looked delighted.

'Oh, you think so?'

'Yeah, you're so trustworthy, you never leave the door outside,' I told him.

The pig was delighted to get a compliment. I'm sure nobody ever complimented them.

'Well, I'm gonna go back to my guard post,' the pig said as he went off, whistling a happy tune.

Whew, that was close. I nodded to Dahlia that she could continue to grope her way towards the keys with the stick. Dahlia concentrated. The stick had reached the keys. Yes! She hooked the keys with the end of the stick. Now she was guiding the stick towards me. The keys were

getting closer to my cage door, and the stick
was trembling because Dahlia was so nervous.
I heard noises coming from outside the door
again. It couldn't be Gale, could it? Hurry up,
Dahlia! The doorknob turned. The keys were so
close! The door opened and the keys dropped to
the floor just a few centimetres from the cage.
Gale entered the room.

'Why are the keys on the floor?' Gale raged.

I had to stay calm so our plan wouldn't be
revealed.

'There was a slight earthquake just now, and
they fell off the hook,' I explained.

Gale thought for a moment.

'I don't believe you. Guard pig, get in here!'
she commanded.

The guard pig appeared.

'What's wrong?' he asked.

'Was the prisoner moving around?' Gale
demanded.

The pig pondered.

'Well, yeah. She was playing around like a flowerpot, like this.' The guard pig demonstrated how I had wobbled from side to side, and then he bumped into Gale's real flowerpot, which fell right on his head.

'You numbskull!' Gale shouted in anger.

OINK!

'Sorry,' the pig said with the flowerpot on his head.

'Get out of my sight!' Gale screamed.

'OK, I'll get out of your sight,' the pig said, bumping into the walls as he left.

Gale checked the lock on the cage. 'Yep, it's still locked. Maybe you are telling the truth.'

Then she placed the keys underneath her bed.

'Of course I'm telling the truth. I never lie,' I lied.

There was a knock-knock-knock at the door. And now Gale lost her patience. She leaped off the bed, as furious as a wasp that had crashed into a tree.

'That's it! I want a real palace of my own, with a moat and a huge iron gate so I don't have to suffer this constant knocking! I'm not going to open it! Get away from my door, whoever you are,' Gale yelled.

I was sure it was one of the girls attempting to rescue me. Somebody had to open that door.

'Open the door – it might be good news,' I ventured.

'No way, I'm Princess Gale, and I'm not opening any more doors,' she snapped.

'Princess Temper Tantrum,' I whispered to myself.

'What did you say, caged bird?' Gale asked.

'Nothing.'

Even toddlers having temper tantrums are smarter than Gale.

'Maybe THIS TIME the pigs found your treasure?' I tried to persuade her to open the door. I could see she was uncertain.

'Do you think so?' she asked.

I could see Gale was thinking it over.

'All right, that's it! I'm coming!' Gale exclaimed. She opened the door, and there was Willow! Without a disguise.

'Oh look, it's the old drama queen in a hat,' Gale said with a nasty laugh.

I looked at Willow in amazement. No disguise!

'Gale, please listen. Let Stella out of prison,' she said, giving Gale a sad look with her head tilted.

'Why should I let her out?' I could see how cruel Gale looked. This was a really dumb plan for the girls to have come up with.

'Because Stella's suffering. Let her come home with us, and we'll never bother you again.'

Willow was looking deep into Gale's eyes. She was trying to hypnotise Gale! Brilliant!

'Stella's suffering – she can't be herself. In honour of your old friendship, please let Stella go free. I know you have a good heart,' Willow said, moved by her own words.

A tear came to Gale's eye, too. She took the keys and came towards my cage with them. This might work!

'You're right, Willow. I do have a good heart,' Gale said.

'Yay, am I going to be freed?' I exclaimed.

'You're so awesome, Gale. I knew you had that goodness inside you,' Willow smiled.

Gale put the key in the lock.

'Thank you for saying that, Willow. You really made me think about how selfish I was being,' Gale said as she turned the key. 'Wait, I'll open the door all the way so you can get out,' she added, and opened the door to the cage.

Just as I was getting out, Gale screamed.

'Oh no, a flying tuna with the eyes of a crab!' she shrieked.

'Where?' Willow and I exclaimed in unison and looked over to the window. Then Gale shoved Willow into the cage too and slammed the door shut. Gale laughed until tears came to her eyes.

'You meanie!' I yelled.

Gale cackled.

'Did you actually think I was that stupid?' she snapped.

'Gale, don't do this,' Willow pleaded.

'Flying tuna! What simple-minded caged birds. Of course I knew all along who you intruders are,' Gale mocked.

'You'll regret this,' I fumed and kicked the cage.

'No one will stop my digging operations,' Gale announced.

'Let me out!' Willow yelled.

'Come on, think positive. Now the caged bird has a companion. Ah, this is so invigorating. Now I can go and continue my work,' Gale sneered. She let out a cackle as she left.

Uh-oh!

'Stella, are we ever gonna get out of here?' Willow asked.

'Of course we are,' I reassured my friend, even though I wasn't sure at all.

Willow is such a sensitive soul, and she always thinks the best of people.

'Maybe Gale didn't mean it that way. Maybe this cage is her guest bed,' Willow ventured, but we both knew that wasn't true.

The next day, Willow and I were still feeling down in the dumps. There were two of us in the cage, and Gale was nowhere to be seen. We were running out of options.

'Stella, I'm scared,' Willow said.

'Oh, we'll make it. By the way, how did you guys find me?' I asked.

'We missed you so much, we went out looking for you,' Willow said in a sad voice.

'But you weren't even my friends anymore,' I retorted.

Willow was confused. 'What do you mean?' she asked.

'You were doing your own thing and didn't invite me along. Plus, you lied to me,' I said. It felt good to get things off my chest.

Willow had a really strange expression.

'But that ...' she began, but then Gale returned. Willow hid underneath her hat.

'Pretty soon, I'll be the ruler of the whole world,' Gale shrieked.

'Queen Nutcase the First,' I muttered to myself.

Gale glared at me. 'Now, now, don't grumble, Stella dear,' she said as she started running water for a bath.

'You'd be in a bad mood if you were locked up in jail,' I snarled at Gale.

Gale gave me a nasty look, just as Willow decided to tune in, peeking out from under her hat.

'Don't make her mad,' Willow whispered.

Gale went over to my backpack.

'Before my bath, I think I'll check out what's in here. A caged bird doesn't need any possessions,' she said, chuckling sarcastically.

Oh no, she was going to find my speaky! I should have used it to call for more backup while I had the chance …

Then I had a flash of inspiration. Eureka! I'm a genius! All I had to do was get Gale to press the green button on the speaky.

'Oh yes, your highness, that's very wise,' I said, pretending to be humble.

'Now, that sounds good,' Gale said as she dug around in my backpack.

'Thank you, your highness.'

I continued my humble act when Gale picked up the speaky. 'Oh, your highness, if you press the green button on that device, it produces beauty-enhancing microwave rays,' I told her.

Gale inspected the speaky. 'I don't believe it,' she said.

'Oh, you can believe it. Dahlia built it. She's so talented,' I assured her.

Gale was interested now, so she pressed the button. 'Might as well try it out,' she said, looking excited.

'And now hold it up to your face,' I told her.

And Gale raised it up. 'I can already feel how much it's doing for my skin,' she squealed.

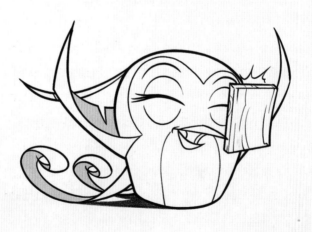

'You're getting more beautiful before our very eyes!' I said.

'Oh, it feels lovely,' Gale shrieked.

Willow looked at me in amazement.

'Princess Gale?' I said.

'What is it, my little caged bird?' she replied.

'It's just that there is one marvellous palace on the island. It has a big iron gate and a moat. Nobody can get in by knocking or asking the person who lives there for entry. Its floor sparkles, as if there were some treasure hidden there,' I told her.

Gale was excited. 'Where is it?' she asked.

'I'll tell you soon, your highness. It's near where our stage is, where Lady Gale performed,' I tried to explain as clearly as possible, so that Dahlia and Poppy would hear on the other end of the line. Now Willow realised what I was up to.

'I wanna go there!' Gale squealed.

'You'll get there. It's made for you!' I assured her.

'All right, I think that's enough beautifying,' she said.

'No! Keep going!' I blurted out – I hadn't said everything I needed to say yet. 'You want to be sure you're at your most beautiful when you find the treasure in the palace. You should use it for a little while longer.'

'I want to move there now!' Gale announced.

'Not now, while it's night-time. In daylight you'll see the whole palace in all its glory – plus, it's easier to move,' I explained.

Gale thought it over. 'Maybe you're right. Tomorrow I'll move all my stuff there and get the treasure. And you two birds will also go to live there, in a little cage up by the ceiling,' she said.

Ugh. Now I just had to hope Dahlia and Poppy took the hint and were building some kind of trap. At least we'd get out of here tomorrow. That was nice, because I really missed being outdoors.

'Oh – one more thing. If there's no palace and no treasure, I'll make you two into fricassee and feed you to the fish!' Gale said and turned away.

'That sounds fair,' I said, playing it cool, even though I was a little concerned. If Dahlia and Poppy weren't listening, we were going to have a problem. Actually, we already did, because they only had one night to come up with something. Willow was freaking out. She's so incredibly sensitive. I gave her a hug to comfort her and said everything would work out. After all, I'm the brave one!

I didn't sleep a wink. I was so nervous about how things would turn out.

'Stella, I'm scared,' Willow whispered.

'I know, but let's not let the fear get the better of us,' I replied.

'How come you went into the forest in the first place?' she asked.

Now I could come right out and tell her.

'Because you guys abandoned me and lied to me about a bunch of stuff. That's not a nice thing for friends to do,' I said.

Willow was horrified.

'Oh, no! Is that really what you thought?'

'I didn't *think* anything. You were really mean to me, so I figured I'd leave,' I told her. I saw Willow's horrified expression. That's really how I felt they had treated me.

'But we just wanted to ...' Willow stopped mid-sentence, as if she had just remembered something.

'What?' I asked.

'Oh, nothing,' Willow said and looked away.

Well, well. Willow was giving me more of the same. When we got out of there, I wasn't going to rejoin the others, I was going to head to the other side of the island.

As the new day dawned, Gale bounced out of bed.

'Woo-hoo! Today's the day I move into my palace and get my treasure!' she exclaimed as she opened the curtains.

'I dreamed I was being held prisoner by a crazy princess, and ...' Willow clammed up when she saw Gale putting on a crown and regal gown, and then added: 'That was no dream.'

'I'm absolutely sure the girls got our message. It'll all work out,' I reassured her, even though I wasn't sure at all, to tell the truth. Poppy and

Dahlia would've had to build an entire palace overnight, plus some kind of trap that would save Willow and me from our miserable fate.

TOOOOT! Gale blew into a big horn, and footsteps sounded outside the door. The door opened, and the guard pig brought a big cage to Gale.

'Here is the travel cage you asked for,' he said in an official voice.

'Put those drips in it,' Gale ordered.

'Yes, princess,' the pig replied.

And then a herd of pigs lifted Willow and me into the cage and placed the cage on two wooden poles, which they used to carry us.

'And now, over to the treasure,' Gale said excitedly.

On our way to the palace, Willow and I were bouncing around inside the cage.

I heard one pig ask another pig, 'How come that bird's wearing a hat?'

'Maybe she's cold,' the second pig replied.

'But it's warm here,' a third pig said.

'Maybe she's cold then,' a fourth pig remarked.

'Quiet there,' Gale barked.

'Yes, Mr... Mrs... Miss Princess,' the pigs replied.

'Now sing! Sing!' Gale commanded. She started.

Gale's the ruler of the world!
Gale's the ruler of the world, the pigs echoed.
All the others are rubbish!
All the others are rubbish, the pigs bellowed.
Gale's the princess of our isle!
Gale's the princess of our isle, the pigs chanted.

Soon, we had reached the right spot. I was totally
stressed out. Everything depended on this.

And there it was. We had reached our band
stage, only it wasn't just a stage – it was now a
real palace! And there was a big iron door at
the front! How on earth did Poppy and Dahlia
put this together? The palace was just beautiful.
Its front wall stood on our former stage. It was
painted, and the floor was gleaming and golden.
There's just no way they could have done all that
in one night! How was that possible? The whole
procession came to a stop.

'This is awesome! A totally amazing palace!
And there's the treasure!' Gale shrieked and
hurried up the red carpet towards the door.

The pigs placed us on the ground and ran after Gale, leaving the key hanging from our cage in their excitement. At that moment, Dahlia raced over to us, took the key and opened the cage.

'Let's move it!' Dahlia shouted, but there was no danger.

Gale was so enchanted by the palace, she was no longer paying attention to us. We stayed to watch what was happening.

'Here comes the princess!' But she didn't notice that there was no palace but simply a scenery panel with shiny paper underneath. When she opened the door, she fell into the stream flowing directly behind the stage. First Gale fell in, then a couple of pigs. The rest of the pigs thought they'd join them for a swim and leaped into the fast-flowing water.

'This doesn't end here, Stella, you traitorrrr!' Gale yelled as the current carried her away. Some of the pigs were crying, others were screaming. They had no idea what was going on.

'Bye-bye, Gale, have a nice swim!' I laughed.

We were safe.

'You guys are geniuses, Dahlia and Poppy!' I exclaimed. And we were all relieved.

In the evening, we all sat around the campfire and recalled what had happened.

'How come you went away, Stella?' Dahlia asked.

'Because you guys weren't my friends anymore,' I replied.

Everybody looked at me in amazement.

'What do you mean?' Poppy asked, shocked.

'You kept on lying to me, and you were always up to something,' I explained.

'But –' Willow stammered.

'I felt really miserable and alone, even though we had just said that friendship oath,' I said, as a tear fell from my cheek onto the campfire.

Dahlia cleared her throat. 'Look, Stella. We were putting together a surprise for you,' she explained.

'What surprise?' I asked between sobs.

'A new stage. We had to keep you out of the way so you wouldn't see it,' Dahlia added.

'Is that true?' I asked.

'Yep. First we had to keep you away from the beach while we were trying to find washed-up nails for our stage. Then we had to keep you away from the stage while we were reinforcing it. Last of all, Willow decorated it, and we were

planning how we were going to surprise you,'
Dahlia explained.

'So that's why you had a picture of me in a
blindfold?' I asked.

'Yeah, we would have taken your blindfold
off near the stage, and we thought it was such a
great idea, we imagined how surprised you'd be,'
Willow said.

'So that's why you were laughing. I thought you were making fun of me,' I said.

'No, definitely not,' Poppy said.

That explained why the palace was so impressive. They couldn't possibly have built it in one night, not even Dahlia. In fact, it was our new stage, and they'd been building it in secret.

'We wanted to give you a nice surprise, because you're the soul of our band, and the old stage was so wobbly,' Poppy added.

'How did you come up with the palace wall?' I asked.

'When we heard you over the speaky, we came up with a solution. We remembered Willow had that backdrop from the scenery for her play. We got it out of storage and rolled out a red carpet. Finally, we put some shiny gold paper on the floor. Then it was all smooth sailing,' Poppy explained.

'You guys are amazing,' I said in awe.

'Shall we go check out the new stage?' Dahlia asked.

I was so happy. Nobody had abandoned me.

We got up on the new stage and the whole band played together again.

I was so happy. I am happy! I love my friends!

ANGRY BIRDS™
Stella

DON'T MISS
THE OTHER BOOKS IN THIS
EXCITING,
NEW SERIES!

ANGRY BIRDS™
Stella
DIARIES

WILLOW
TAKES THE STAGE

EGMONT

STELLA, DAHLIA, POPPY, WILLOW AND LUCA:

ANGRY BIRDS™ Stella DIARIES

POPPY'S PERFECT PRANK

EGMONT

BEST FRIENDS FOREVER... MOST OF THE TIME!

EGMONT